Bun Bun Button

Patricia Polacco

G. P. Putnam's Sons
An Imprint of Penguin Group (USA) Inc.

To the Zajack family: Paige Elizabeth, Jordyn Palma and Olivia Katharine

Patricia Lee Gauch, Editor

G. P. PUTNAM'S SONS · A division of Penguin Young Readers Group.
Published by The Penguin Group.
Penguin Group (USA) Inc., 375 Hudson Street, New York, NY 10014, U.S.A.
Penguin Group (Canada), 90 Eglinton Avenue East, Suite 700, Toronto, Ontario M4P 2Y3, Canada (a division of Pearson Penguin Canada Inc.).
Penguin Books Ltd, 80 Strand, London WC2R 0RL, England.
Penguin Ireland, 25 St. Stephen's Green, Dublin 2, Ireland (a division of Penguin Books Ltd.).
Penguin Group (Australia), 250 Camberwell Road, Camberwell, Victoria 3124, Australia (a division of Pearson Australia Group Pty Ltd).
Penguin Books India Pvt Ltd, 11 Community Centre, Panchsheel Park, New Delhi - 110 017, India.
Penguin Group (NZ), 67 Apollo Drive, Rosedale, North Shore 0632, New Zealand (a division of Pearson New Zealand Ltd).
Penguin Books (South Africa) (Pty) Ltd, 24 Sturdee Avenue, Rosebank, Johannesburg 2196, South Africa.
Penguin Books Ltd, Registered Offices: 80 Strand, London WC2R 0RL, England.

Design by Semadar Megged.   Text set in 16-point Adobe Jenson.   The illustrations are rendered in pencils and markers.
Library of Congress Cataloging-in-Publication Data is available upon request.

ISBN 978-0-399-25472-7
Special Markets ISBN 978-0-399-25576-2 Not for resale
1 3 5 7 9 10 8 6 4 2

This Imagination Library edition is published by Penguin Group (USA), a Pearson
company, exclusively for Dolly Parton's Imagination Library, a not-for-profit
program designed to inspire a love of reading and learning, sponsored in part by The
Dollywood Foundation. Penguin's trade editions of this work are available wherever
books are sold.

Bun Bun Button

Patricia Polacco

G. P. Putnam's Sons
An Imprint of Penguin Group (USA) Inc.

Paige Elizabeth Darling adored her gramma. When Paige visited—which was often—Gramma let Paige help bake soft sand cookies, make the beds and feed the kitties and the dogs.

And when Paige was done, she and Gramma would climb into the Old Blue Chair which they loved and cuddle and read.

Everybody at Gramma's house loved that chair. Her five kitties did. The dogs did. Her gramma's pet squirrel did. Even Gramma's goldfish did!

Sometimes it got a little crowded.

According to Gramma, the secret of that Old Blue Chair was that it soaked up so much love from all of them that it spilled all over whoever was sitting in it.

"Aren't we lucky to have this chair, Gramma," Paige would say.

"We're Darlings, and we Darlings have always been lucky!" Gramma would purr.

One day, as Paige sat in the Old Blue Chair, she found herself thinking something was missing. When the kitties and the dogs and the squirrel sat in the chair, they each had toys that Gramma had made just for them. Everyone except Paige.

"Gramma, can you make something for me to hold when I'm in the Old Blue Chair?" Paige asked one day.

Gramma smiled. "I have the perfect little something in mind to sew just for you." She dug deep into her calico chest and pulled out some cloth. That night, she cut and pinned and stitched, working long after Paige was in bed.

The next morning, there right next to her pillow was the most beautiful stuffed bunny she had ever seen. Paige hugged her next to her heart.

"I'm going to call her Bun Bun Button!" Paige whispered.

"And did you see the tiny little pocket in her right ear for your finger when you nuzzle her into your face?" Gramma asked.

Sure enough, there it was. Paige nestled Bun Bun into her cheek, put her favorite finger into the stuffed bunny's ear pocket and cuddled and cuddled.

Bun Bun Button went everywhere with Paige. She rode in
Paige's special doll buggy, watched while Paige waded in the
rubber pool under the Sleeping Willow, sat with Paige by
the birdbath.

At night, when Paige climbed into bed, she felt the softness of the pocket
in Bun Bun's ear and held her close until they both grew very sleepy.

One sunny day, as they were on a walk together, Paige and her gramma came upon a big round man selling big round balloons. Paige's gramma picked out the biggest, reddest one for her darling granddaughter.

Walking home, that balloon tugged at the string. "It wants to fly, Gramma," Paige sang out.

"It's filled with helium," Gramma said. "If you let that string go, it will float up and far away."

When they got home, Paige tied the balloon to Bun Bun's arm. Sure enough, when she let go of the string, Bun Bun floated up to the ceiling.

"Look—Bun Bun Button wants to fly, too!"

"Don't take that balloon outside with Bun Bun tied to it," her gramma warned. "You know what will happen if you let go!"

"But Gramma, Bun Bun wants to see the sky," Paige pleaded. "Tie the string around my wrist." Paige held on to the string, too, just in case, and went outside with Bun Bun.

Bun Bun and Paige danced around the backyard together. They ran around the birdbath, bounced under the Sleeping Willow, skipped around the lilac bush.

The string was tied to Paige's wrist and Bun Bun was perfectly safe. But then she jumped the privet hedge. The string got caught and came untied.

Up, up, up the balloon went—and Bun Bun with it.

It floated up past the birdbath, around the fountain, and, finally, up past the Sleeping Willow tree.

"Gramma!" Paige cried, but then a big gust of wind came and blew the balloon higher and higher until the balloon and Bun Bun disappeared into the clouds.

That night, even in the Old Blue Chair, in her gramma's arms, Paige cried and cried. There was no Bun Bun to nuzzle as Gramma read to her. No ear pocket to hide her finger in. No soft little round belly to have next to her cheek.

"Do you think Bun Bun will be all right, Gramma? I love her so."

"Maybe a wind will blow her right back here to us," Gramma said. "We Darlings are lucky, after all."

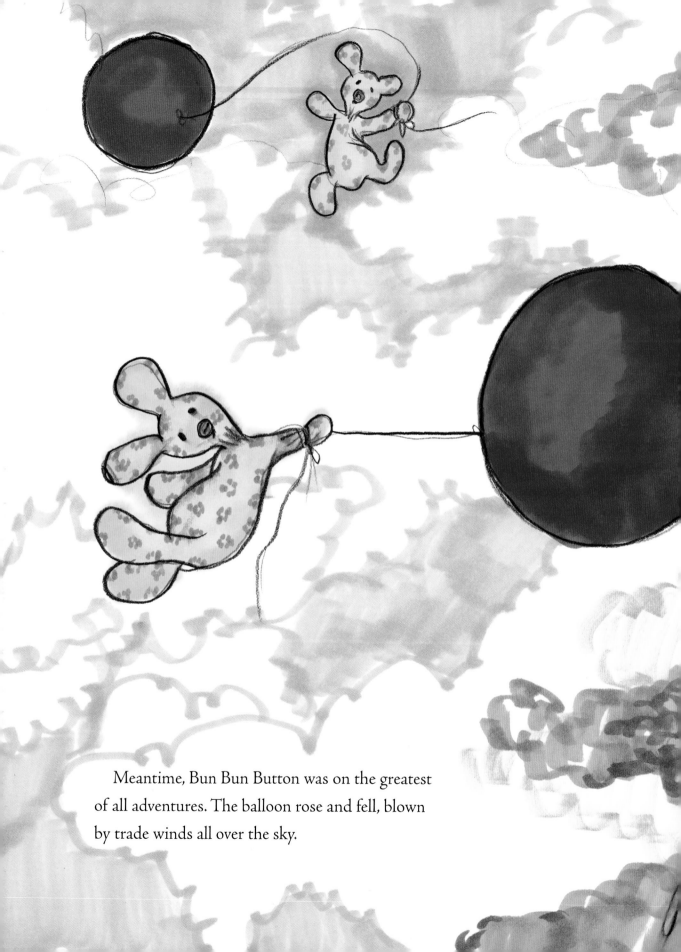

Meantime, Bun Bun Button was on the greatest
of all adventures. The balloon rose and fell, blown
by trade winds all over the sky.

That night, Bun Bun was closer to the stars
than she had ever been.

But when the sun came up, a flock of honking geese flew into Bun Bun and the red balloon, and the string caught in the foot of one of the geese. It honked and flew and pulled Bun Bun along until the string on the balloon broke with a snap.

Bun Bun started to tumble and fall, end over end. The wind whistled through her little ears until Bun Bun landed on the back of a seagull and tumbled toward the ground, down and down . . .

. . . and down. Finally she came to rest on the lowest limb of a willow tree.

There, a squirrel picked Bun Bun up and bounded out of the tree, scampered over the privet hedge, ran under the lilac bush and dropped Bun Bun right at Gramma Darling's feet.

"Oh, pet," Gramma exclaimed. "Where have you been!"

"I'm going to dry you off and mend you good as new."
When she was done, she put her on Paige's pillow to see
when she came over after preschool that day.

Paige came to Gramma's, still very sad. She didn't even want
her sand cookies and milk. She went straight to her room,
and there she saw . . .

"Bun Bun, Bun Bun, you've come back to me!" She scooped
Bun Bun up in her arms.

That night, Gramma, Bun Bun, Paige, the cats, the dogs and the squirrel climbed into the Old Blue Chair together.

"Oh, Gramma, we Darlings are lucky, aren't we," Paige sighed.

"Maybe it's more than luck that brought her back to us, pet. Maybe it was love."

And they all sighed and sipped mint tea and ate soft sand cookies and cuddled deep into the Old Blue Chair together.

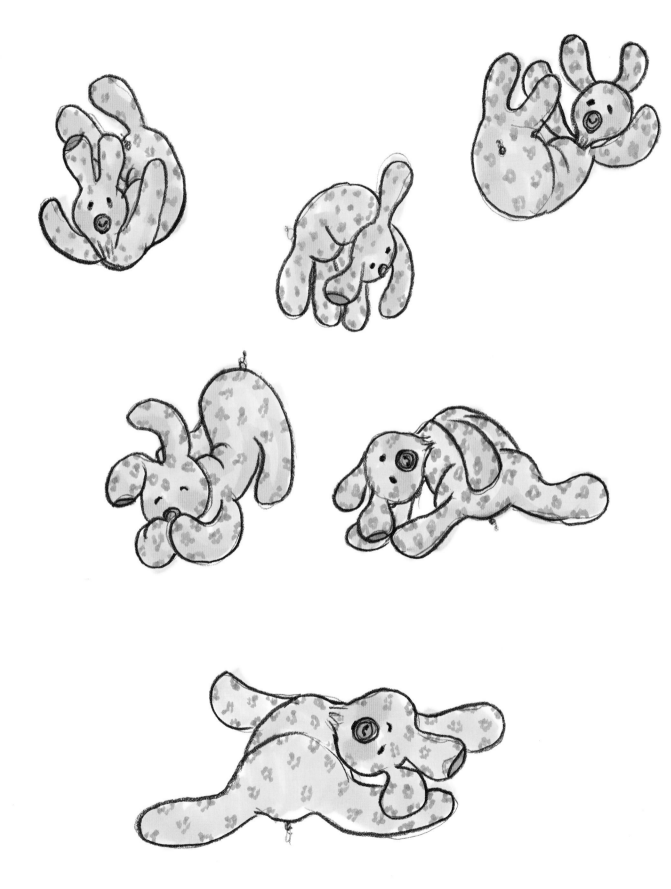